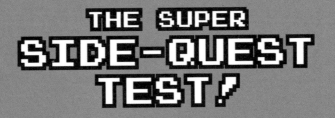

THE SUPER SIDE-QUEST TEST!

READ MORE
PRESS START!
BOOKS!

MORE BOOKS COMING SOON!

PRESS START!

THE SUPER SIDE-QUEST TEST!

THOMAS FLINTHAM

BRANCHES

SCHOLASTIC INC.

FOR RON

Library of Congress Cataloging-in-Publication Data

Names: Flintham, Thomas, author, illustrator. | Flintham, Thomas. Press start! ; 6.
Title: The super side-quest test! / by Thomas Flintham.
Description: New York : Branches/Scholastic Inc., [2019] | Series: Press start! ; 6 | Summary: This time Super Rabbit Boy will need the power of the Mega Wand to defeat the evil King Viking—but first he must go on a seemingly endless series of quests before he can obtain the wand and save the day.
Identifiers: LCCN 2018024388 | ISBN 9781338239782 (pbk.) | ISBN 9781338239799 (jacketed hardcover)
Subjects: LCSH: Superheroes—Juvenile fiction. | Supervillains—Juvenile fiction. | Magic wands—Juvenile fiction. | Video games—Juvenile fiction. | Animals—Juvenile fiction. | CYAC: Superheroes—Fiction. | Supervillains—Fiction. | Magic wands—Fiction. | Video games—Fiction. | Animals—Fiction.
Classification: LCC PZ7.1.F585 Sy 2019 | DDC [Fic]—dc23 LC record available at https://https://lccn.loc.gov/2018024388

10 9 8 7 6 5 4 3 2 1   19 20 21 22 23

Printed in China   38
First edition, January 2019
Edited by Celia Lee
Book design by Maria Mercado

TABLE OF CONTENTS

Meanie King Viking is taking over Animal Town again! He is using a Mega Giant Super Robot to cause trouble.

Hero Super Rabbit Boy is ready to stop King Viking. He rushes to the town.

Super Rabbit Boy leaps into action.

The Mega Giant Super Robot moves really quickly! Super Rabbit Boy tries to dodge it.

Super Rabbit Boy is trapped! King Viking is pleased.

Ha! Ha! You're not fast enough to beat my Mega Giant Super Robot! Now it's your turn to blast off!

The Mega Giant Super Robot tosses Super Rabbit Boy far, far away!

Oh noooooooooo!

Bye, Smelly Rabbit Boy!

Super Rabbit Boy lands far, far, far away from Animal Town. But he needs to make it back home. So he sets off on an epic quest. Along the way, he faces:

a giant dragon,

a band of pinklings,

and a Snobble ghoul.

He also finds his way through the Tunnels of Gloom.

And he solves the mystery of the fake queen.

At long last, Super Rabbit Boy sees Animal Town. It doesn't look good.

I'll stop you, King Viking! Boing! Boing! Here I come!

Keep going, Super Rabbit Boy! You're almost there!

Super Rabbit Boy is so close to Animal Town. King Viking's Robot Army waits for him.

Super Rabbit Boy leaps into action.

Boing! Boing! You can't stop me!

Soon, Super Rabbit Boy has beaten all the robots! Animal Town is steps away.

That Mega Giant Super Robot is so powerful. How can I beat it?

Maybe I can help you.

Super Rabbit Boy turns around. He sees a very friendly person.

Hello, little hero! I am Dave the Traveling Salesman. I have an item to help you with your problem.

13

Super Rabbit Boy is worried. He is so close to home, but he isn't sure if he can beat the Mega Giant Super Robot.

Find those gold coins, Super Rabbit Boy!

3 THE SEARCH FOR GOLD

Super Rabbit Boy starts his search for the three gold coins at his home, Carrot Castle.

Super Rabbit Boy searches the whole castle for some coins. Finally, he has some luck.

He searches every little space. He doesn't find more gold coins. But he does find a treasure map.

Super Rabbit Boy sets off. He follows the trail on the treasure map and runs as fast as he can.

Super Rabbit Boy finds a big rock with a "X" on it. He picks it up.

It's another coin! Hooray!

I need one more gold coin to get the Mega Wand. I need to hurry. Animal Town needs my help!

Super Rabbit Boy dashes down the mountain. On the way, he spots a girl. She looks upset!

The girl is a slime farmer, but all her slimes have run away.

Don't worry! I will help you catch them.

Thank you! If you find them all, I'll give you this gold coin.

Super Rabbit Boy springs into action! He quickly finds and scoops up the silly slimes.

Soon, all the slimes are back in their hutch.

Great work!

Super Rabbit Boy gets back to work.

You're almost there, Super Rabbit Boy!

Finally, Super Rabbit Boy puts the last slime back in the hutch. He's very tired and slimy.

At last, Super Rabbit Boy has three gold coins. He can buy the Mega Wand!

Dave the Traveling Salesman is waiting in the field for Super Rabbit Boy.

Dave gives Super Rabbit Boy the Mega Wand. Now he can save Animal Town.

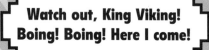

Watch out, King Viking! Boing! Boing! Here I come!

It's time to test out the Mega Wand.
Super Rabbit Boy swooshes it around.

Nothing happens!

Hey! It isn't working.

Of course not!

Why not?

There is a sign on Dave's pack. Dave points to it.

BATTERIES NOT INCLUDED

The Mega Wand uses batteries? I thought it was magic.

28

Super Rabbit Boy needs the Mega Wand to beat King Viking's robot. And he needs batteries to make the Mega Wand work. But does he have time for another side quest?

I'm sure this side quest will be very short. Boing! Boing! Here I go!

Hurry, Super Rabbit Boy! Animal Town needs help right away.

Super Rabbit Boy runs to Billy Bob's Everything Shop.

Billy Bob sells all kinds of things. He must have some batteries!

BILLY BOB'S EVERYTHING SHOP!!!!!!!!!!

Billy Bob is outside his shop. He's locked out!

Billy Bob tells Super Rabbit Boy that he went on a walk in the Wobbly Woods. He must have dropped his key there.

Don't worry, Billy Bob. I'll find your key!

In the Wobbly Woods, Super Rabbit Boy starts searching for the key.

I hope this search doesn't take too long.

He searches the floor of the whole woods, but he can't find the key.

Where could it be?

Suddenly, he spots a glimmer high up in one of the trees.

Super Rabbit Boy starts to climb the tree.

He jumps from tree branch to tree branch, higher and higher.

It's Angie Crow. She is not happy with Super Rabbit Boy!

CAW! CAW! YOU SNEAKY SNEAK! THIS KEY IS MINE!

Super Rabbit Boy tells Angie Crow about Billy Bob and his lost key.

Oh no! Will this side quest ever end?

6 MORE TO DO

Super Rabbit Boy's side quest for the batteries is tricky. He searches high and low for a new shiny thing to give to the crow. His search brings him to the beach.

Super Rabbit Boy spots something shining out at sea.

He jumps into the water and swims toward the flickering light.

Super Rabbit Boy tells Maria about the Wand, the batteries, and Angie Crow. He tells her how he needs something shiny to get Billy Bob's key from the crow.

43

I just need something else for my hair. Then the pearl clip is yours!
I'll see what I can do.

This side quest is getting so silly!

Back on the beach, Super Rabbit Boy starts his search. It's not easy!

I have to hurry.

Suddenly, Super Rabbit Boy hears a cry. It sounds scary! What could it be?

Wah! Wah!
Wwwaaaaaaahhhhhh!

Super Rabbit Boy follows the crying sound. He soon finds a very loud and very mad little girl. Her dad looks very stressed.

Oh dear! What is wrong?

Super Rabbit Boy has an idea.

Super Rabbit Boy's quest is getting bigger and bigger.

Soon, Super Rabbit Boy finds a small gerblin with a toy. But the gerblin won't give the toy to him. The gerblin wants to go on a big adventure. And he needs a helmet to keep him safe.

Gerble gerb! You can have my toy if you give me a helmet.

Super Rabbit Boy spots a bucket floating down a river. It would make a good helmet for the gerblin. He dives into the water to grab it.

This water is really fast!

Oh no! There is a waterfall up ahead.
Be careful, Super Rabbit Boy!

8 A SUPER QUEST

Super Rabbit Boy grabs the bucket and leaps out of the water. He just misses the waterfall.

At last, Super Rabbit Boy has the bucket.
There is something inside.

What is this?

It's a ghost!

Woooooooo!
You want my bucket?
Find me something else
to hide in!

Super Rabbit Boy sees a monster nearby. She is lifting a big box up and down to make her strong. The box would be a good hiding place for the ghost.

Find me another heavy thing to lift. Then you can have this box. Ra! Ra!

Oh dear. Super Rabbit Boy feels very, very tired. This little side quest has turned into a HUGE side quest.

I need to finish this quest and get back to Animal Town!

You look sad, Super Rabbit Boy! I feel sad, too.

Oh hello, Lazy Susan! Why do you feel sad?

Lazy Susan tells Super Rabbit Boy that she wants to see the world.

But I am too lazy to go anywhere.

Suddenly, Super Rabbit Boy has an idea!

I think I can solve both of our problems, Lazy Susan.

Uh-oh, Lazy Susan has fallen asleep. You better have a good idea, Super Rabbit Boy!

9 SOMETHING FOR EVERYONE

Super Rabbit Boy picks up Lazy Susan. They race back to the monster.

I hope this works. I need those batteries!

Super Rabbit Boy gives Lazy Susan to the monster. He asks the monster to carry Lazy Susan on a trip around the world.

I'm going to get super strong! Ra! Ra!

World Trip! Yay! Zzzzz . . .

Now the monster does not need the big box. She gives it to Super Rabbit Boy.

The ghost is very happy to swap the bucket for the big box.

Super Rabbit Boy gives his bucket to the gerblin. He loves the bucket helmet! He gives Super Rabbit Boy his new toy.

The little girl stops crying when she sees her new toy. Her dad is so happy! He starts to cry instead.

Thank you so much! Here is the hair ribbon.

Weee!

Super Rabbit Boy gives Maria the Mermaid the hair ribbon.

This is perfect! It will help keep my hair dry.

She gives Super Rabbit Boy the pearl hair clip.

I hope this clip is shiny enough for Angie Crow!

Angie Crow is very happy with the pearl hair clip!

At last, Super Rabbit Boy has the key he needs to open Billy Bob's Everything Shop!

Hooray! Super Rabbit Boy finally has the batteries for his Mega Wand! But his side quest took a <u>long</u> time. Animal Town still still needs his help!

Boing! Boing! Here I come!

Super Rabbit Boy is back in Animal Town. The Mega Giant Super Robot has been busy!

Oh no! Animal Town is a mess!

He pops the batteries into the Mega Wand.

King Viking is mad.

Super Rabbit Boy holds up the Mega Wand. It starts to glow.

A huge blast of battery-powered energy bursts from the Mega Wand. It sends King Viking and his Mega Giant Super Robot flying!

It's my turn to pick you up and throw you away!

BOOP!

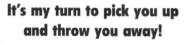

Animal Town is safe once again, but it's a bit of a mess.

Suddenly, the Mega Wand starts to glow!

The Mega Wand's power quickly fixes the town.

Thank you!

Well, that was easy!

THOMAS FLINTHAM

has always loved to draw and tell stories, and now that is his job! He grew up in Lincoln, England, and studied illustration in Camberwell, London. He lives by the sea with his wife, Bethany, in Cornwall.

Thomas is the creator of THOMAS FLINTHAM'S BOOK OF MAZES AND PUZZLES and many other books for kids. PRESS START! is his first early chapter book series.

OH NO! Billy Bob has lost his key again! Can you help him find it?

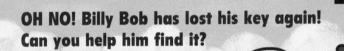

PRESS START!

How much do you know about
THE SUPER SIDE-QUEST TEST!?

What are some of the mini adventures Super Rabbit Boy has on the way back to Animal Town?

Why can't Super Rabbit Boy use the Mega Wand?

Look at the picture on page 32. What is happening to Billy Bob's key?

How does Super Rabbit Boy feel before and after the quest for the batteries?

Super Rabbit Boy meets many people in the story. Who is your favorite? Use words and pictures to explain.

scholastic.com/branches

31901064099924